Bilingual Edition

READING POWER

Edición Bilingüe

Kobe Bryant

"Slam Dunk" Champion

Campeón del "Slam Dunk"

Rob Kirkpatrick

Traducción al español
Mauricio Velázquez de León

The Rosen Publishing Group's
PowerKids Press™ & Buenas Letras™
New York

For my sister, Casey.
Para mi hermana Casey.

Published in 2002 by The Rosen Publishing Group, Inc.
29 East 21st Street, New York, NY 10010

First Bilingual Edition 2002
First Edition in English 2001

Book Design: Michael de Guzman

Photo Credits: pp. 5, 22 © Andrew D. Bernstein/NBA/Allsport; pp. 7, 15, 21 © Todd Warshaw/Allsport; p. 9 © David Taylor/Allsport; p. 11 © Vincent Laforet/Allsport; p. 13 © Tom Hauck/Allsport; p. 17 © Brian Bahr/Allsport; p. 19 © Aubrey Washington/Allsport.

Text Consultant: Linda J. Kirkpatrick, Reading Specialist/Reading Recovery Teacher

Kirkpatrick, Rob.
  Kobe Bryant : "slam dunk" champion = Kobe Bryant : campeón del "slam dunk"/ by Rob Kirkpatrick : traducción al español Mauricio Velázquez de León.
    p. cm. — (Reading power)
  Includes index.
  SUMMARY: Introduces Kobe Bryant, a young player for the Los Angeles Lakers basketball team.
  ISBN 0-8239-6142-7 (lib. bdg.)
  1. Bryant, Kobe, 1978– Juvenile literature. 2. Basketball players—United States Biography Juvenile literature. [1. Bryant, Kobe, 1978– 2. Basketball players. 3. Afro-Americans—Biography. 4. Spanish language materials—Bilingual.] I. Title. II. Series.
  GV884.B794 K57 1999
  796.323'092—dc21
  [B]

Word Count:
English: 124
Spanish: 136

Manufactured in the United States of America

Contents

Contenido

Kobe Bryant plays basketball. He is in the NBA.

———

Kobe Bryant juega baloncesto *(basketball)*. Él juega en la liga NBA.

5

Kobe is on the Los Angeles Lakers. He is number 8.

Kobe juega con los Lakers de Los Ángeles. Él tiene el número 8.

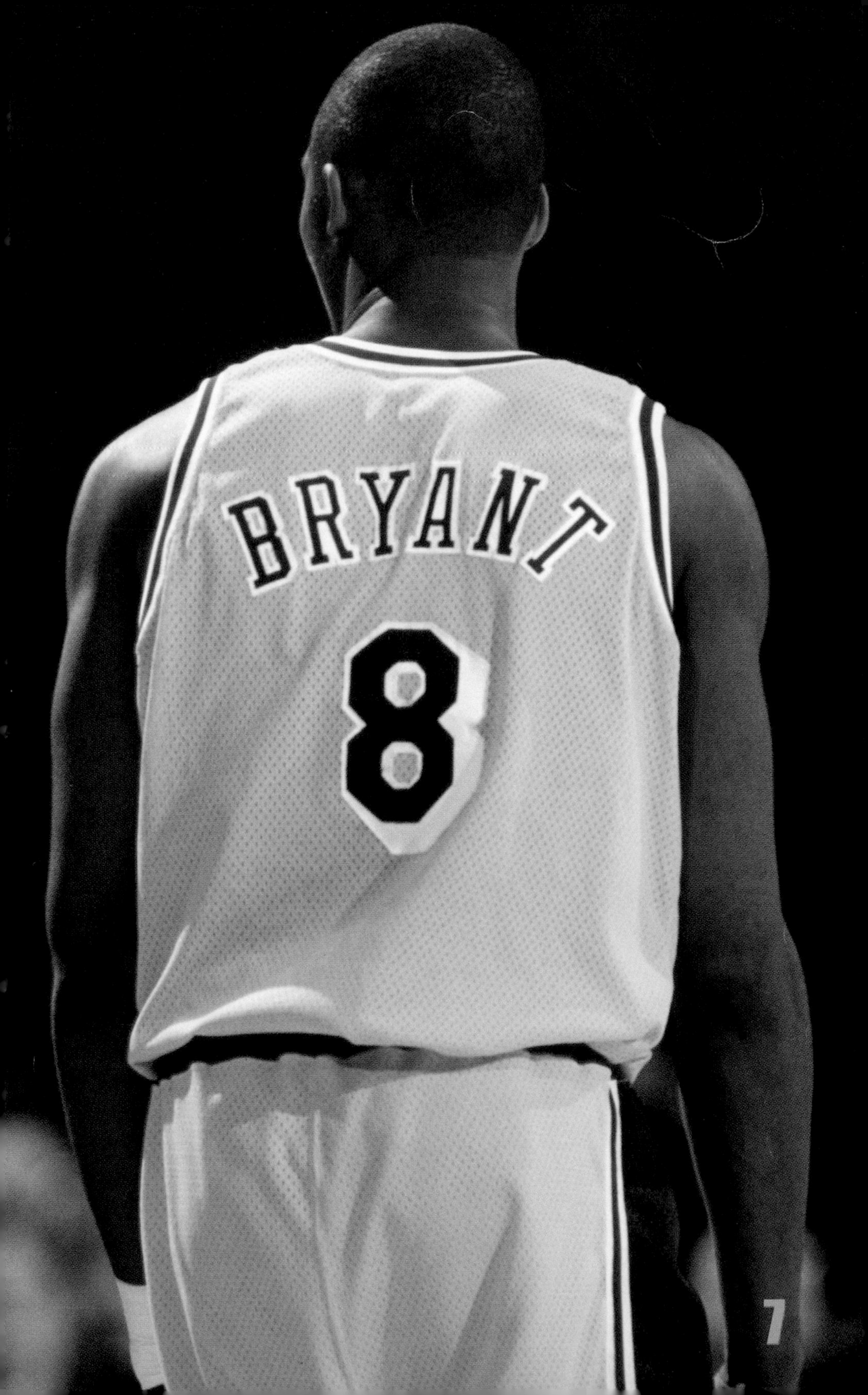
BRYANT
8

Kobe can jump way up in the air.

———————

Kobe puede saltar
muy alto.

Kobe can reach up over players. He jumps high to get to the basket.

———

Kobe puede saltar por encima de otros jugadores. Salta alto para alcanzar la canasta.

Kobe can dunk the ball. He can dunk the ball with one hand. People like to see him dunk the ball.

Kobe puede "clavar" la pelota en la canasta con una sola mano. A los aficionados les gusta cuando la clava. A esto se le llama *Slam Dunk.*

13

Sometimes Kobe uses two hands to dunk the ball.

———

Algunas veces Kobe usa las dos manos para realizar la clavada.

In 1997, Kobe played in an All-Star game. It was a game for rookies. Kobe had a lot of fun.

En 1997, Kobe jugó en el Juego de Estrellas (*All-Star Game*). Fue un partido para novatos. Kobe se divirtió mucho.

Kobe and number 6, Eddie Jones, talked when they played in games.

———————

Kobe y el número 6, Eddie Jones, hablaban durante los partidos.

19

Shaquille O'Neal and Kobe both play for the Lakers.

———

Kobe juega con Shaquille O'Neal en los *Lakers*.

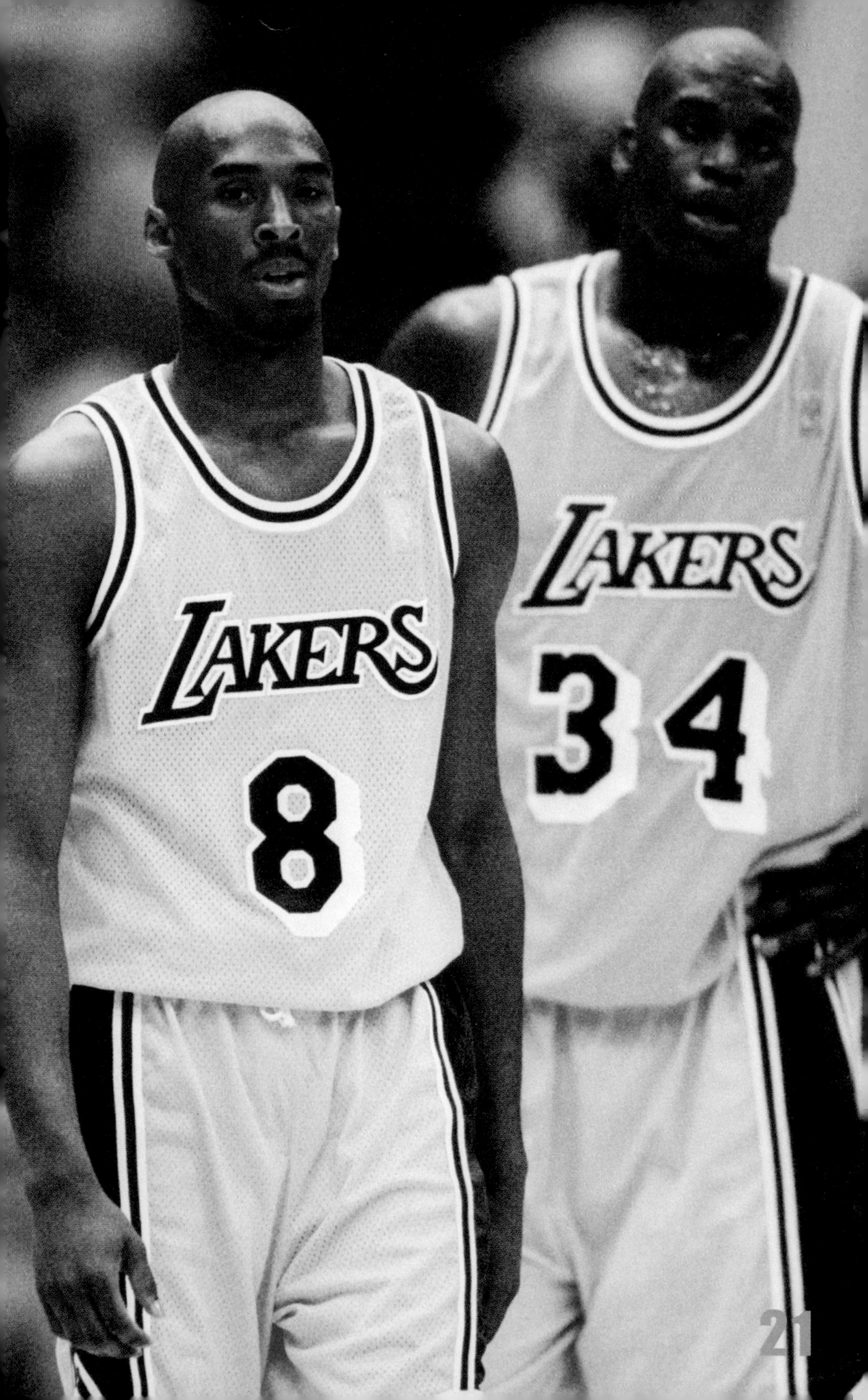
LAKERS
8
LAKERS
34

People like to meet Kobe.
They ask him to write his
name for them.

———————

A la gente le gusta
conocer a Kobe.
Muchas personas le
piden su autógrafo.

Here are more books to read about
Kobe Bryant and basketball:

Para leer más acerca de Kobe Bryant y
baloncesto, te recomendamos estos
libros:

Kobe Bryant, by Richard Brenner
Beach Tree Books (1999)

Basketball ABC: The NBA Alphabet
by Florence Cassen Mayers
Harry N. Abrams (1996)

To learn more about basketball, check
out this Web site:

Para aprender más sobre baloncesto,
visita esta pagina de Internet:

http://www.nba.com/

Glossary

All-Star game (AWL STAR GAYM) A game for very good players.

dunk (DUNK) When a player reaches up and drops the ball right into the basket.

NBA (National Basketball Association) A group of players on different teams who get money to play basketball.

rookies (RUH-keez) New players.

Index

Glosario

Clavada (la) / Slam Dunk Cuando un jugador salta con la bola y la deja caer muy fuerte en la canasta.

Juego de Estrellas (el) / All-Star Game Un partido en el que juegan los mejores jugadores.

Lakers de Los Ángeles Equipo de baloncesto de la ciudad de Los Angeles. *Lakers* quiere decir Laguneros.

NBA (National Basketball Association) Un grupo de jugadores en diferentes equipos a los que se les paga dinero para jugar baloncesto.

novato Jugador nuevo.

Índice